# Fur Is Only Fur Deep

By Julia Schettler
Illustrated By Sarah Neville

Peasantry
PRESS

To Bryan (my super hero) and all our cubs,
Jordan, Jillian, Aubrie, Matthew, Brittany,
Katelynn, Phillip, Kai, and Jayden,
I love you all beary much!
- J. S.

To Chris
and all of my family,
Thank you for your love and support!
- S.N.

*Fur Is Only Fur Deep*
Text Copyright© 2015 by Julia Schettler
Illustrations Copyright© 2015 by Sarah Neville

Published in Canada by PEASANTRY PRESS
Printed in the United States of America

Visit www.peasantrypress.com for information.
Information requests should be addressed to info@peasantrypress.com

ISBN 978-0-9940210-2-1 (pbk.)

PEASANTRY PRESS
Winnipeg, Manitoba, Canada
www.peasantrypress.com

Layout: Peasantry Press
Lead Editor: Francie Humby

*Illustrations done in watercolour and ink on watercolour paper*

Jai Jai was a little panda orphan who lived in the Beary Nice Orphanage.
It was a huge den full of stray panda cubs. Jai Jai liked to print his name "J.J."
His favourite colour was red and his lucky number was three.

Jai Jai was also very curious. He had so many questions it was almost unbearable. "Why am I an orphan?" Jai Jai would ask Teacher Bear. "Why was I left at the front gate? Who left me there?"

"We don't know who left you," Teacher Bear would say with a sigh. "We don't know why they left you, but the gate of the Beary Nice Orphanage was a safe spot to leave you. That shows they loved you," he said, trying, yet again, to reassure Jai Jai.

Jai Jai had two best friends, Mei and Lee. The three cubs were inseparable. The orphanage was the only home they had ever known. They had teachers to teach them, nannies to nanny them, but, sadly, no parents to love them.

Jai Jai and his friends all dreamed of parents. They had even created a game called Furever Family. Every day, they pretended to have perfect panda parents.

Royal pandas always adopted Mei. Her pretend parents were the emperor and empress of the land. Instantly, she became Princess Mei.

Lee's father was a very famous moviemaker. Lee had leading roars in all his shows.

Jai Jai's pretend father was a superhero panda bear. He was super strong, super brave, and super smart. Jai Jai was every panda cub's hero.

Then, one day, everything changed. Teacher Bear took Jai Jai aside, knelt down, and held the cub's little paw. "It's your adoption day. Your new Furever Family is here."

"Here? Today? My new family? My superhero father is here?" Jai Jai stuttered.

Panicked, he raced outside. Other cubs darted out behind him, eager to get a sneak peek.

Jai Jai squinted and stretched up higher on his back paws.

Nothing looked right! The two bears dashing up the path had fur that was all black!

Then Jai Jai saw Teacher Bear shaking the strangers' paws.

Jai Jai sniffed the air. The strange bears smelled different too.

Jai Jai was confused at first. Then he was infuriated!

"Why don't they have any white fur? I want a panda bear mother," he screamed. "Where is my superhero father?" Jai Jai stomped his feet and kicked the grass in a bear cub tantrum.

Teacher Bear clapped his paws loudly three times. Jai Jai stood perfectly still and stopped screaming.

"Your new furever parents promise to love and protect you," Teacher Bear declared. "We are all bears. Fur is only fur deep. It's what's inside a bear that matters."

"I don't care what's inside a black bear," Jai Jai whispered to himself.

Teacher Bear took the strangers on a tour around the orphanage. Jai Jai, Mei, and Lee trailed behind. To Jai Jai, it seemed to take forever! The strangers wanted to see everything. They greeted everyone with a smile and stopped to chat with the cook and the gardener.

Then Teacher Bear led the two black bears down to the front gate. Mother Bear wiped a tear away. Father Bear snapped pictures of the gate.

Jai Jai suddenly shivered. He felt cold and shaky.

"Why do they want pictures of the old front gate?" Lee whispered.

"It was my finding spot," Jai Jai said, choking back tears. "It's the spot where I was found, the place where someone left me."

Silently, Mei and Lee both reached over and held Jai Jai's paws.

Next, the strangers followed Teacher Bear to the orphanage's giant tree. There, the two black bears held Jai Jai's paw and declared, "We promise to give Jai Jai a good home. We will love and protect our new son forever."

Then the black bears signed adoption papers. Jai Jai's adoption was complete. Soon he would be leaving the Beary Nice Orphanage forever. Jai Jai glanced around quickly. There was no superhero anywhere.

Teacher Bear knelt down and gave Jai Jai a new red backpack. It was his very first present! "Don't open this pack until you arrive at your new home. It is full of memories," Teacher Bear said, his voice cracking a little. "I hope we will meet again someday, my little friend." Then Teacher Bear hugged Jai Jai.

As Jai Jai left, Teacher Bear, Mei, and Lee waved goodbye to him.

Tears slid down Jai Jai's face. Mother Bear reached for his paw and squeezed it gently.

Father Bear led the way as they trekked over the mountains. Jai Jai
saw new trails and valleys. Father Bear taught him how to climb tall trees.
Jai Jai was frightened at first, but Father Bear stood right below him,
paws spread out, ready to catch him.

The fast flowing streams scared Jai Jai but Father Bear always held the young cub's paw when they waded into the water. Then, one sunny afternoon, Jai Jai let go of Father's paw. Jai Jai could swim!

Every day, Jai Jai kept waiting for his father to use superhero powers. The panda cub thought maybe his father would fly or climb a steep cliff with a single bound or lift a heavy log with one hand. His father never did.

Day after day, the family plodded along. Whenever Jai Jai got weary, Father gave him a bear-back ride. Whenever Jai Jai got bored, Mother taught him a new song.

Every night, Jai Jai was exhausted, but he was still very curious.
What was in his new red backpack? Frustratingly, Mother Bear was always
hovering close by. How he would have loved to have just one look-see inside!

After many days, the mountains vanished and a forest appeared.
The family had been walking for so long that Jai Jai's paws could barely move.

Suddenly, there was a loud racket. A massive stampede of black bears was racing toward him!

Jai Jai was terrified. Where were Father's super powers?
A superhero would protect him.

Strange black bears would soon be all around him! Father Bear quickly raised his paws, shielding Jai Jai. The stampede halted. Trembling, Jai Jai held his backpack close.

"Meet your new family," Mother Bear shouted above the noise.

"Welcome home! Congratulations!" the black bears roared.

Jai Jai hung onto his father's leg as Father Bear started shaking paws with the stranger black bears. Mother Bear greeted them with hugs.

Everywhere, bears were laughing and cheering. Grandmother bears were finding comfortable spots to rest. Brother Bear, Sister Bear, and cousin bears were smiling at Jai Jai. Delicious bowls of fresh bamboo appeared. Everyone was celebrating Jai Jai's coming home. It was his very first party!

Little Cousin Bear was curious.

"Why does Jai Jai have some white fur?" he asked.

"Bears are all sorts of colours. It's what's inside a cub that matters," Auntie Bear told him. Little Cousin Bear just shrugged. He had no idea what was inside a panda cub.

After awhile, Jai Jai started playing with his new cousins. The cubs were full of get-up-and-go. They did handstands and cartwheels. Jai Jai learned to play hide and seek. Then he taught his cousins a new tag game.

Close to bedtime, all the relatives said goodbye and went home.

Later that night, when the stars were twinkling in the sky, Jai Jai cuddled on his mother's lap. She felt so warm! She smelled so good!

Father Bear handed Jai Jai the backpack. Jai Jai opened it slowly. Inside was a photobook with 'Memories' written on its cover. It was filled with pictures from the Beary Nice Orphanage.

"It's to help you celebrate and remember your past," Mother Bear said softly. "Hopefully, one day, we can return to the orphanage for a visit."

"My friends and I used to play a game called Furever Family. Princess Mei is still waiting for her royal parents," Jai Jai confided. "When Lee is adopted, his father will make him a leading bear in his next movie."

"Mei and Lee are your furever friends," Mother Bear said with a smile.

Jai Jai got down from Mother's lap and crawled up onto Father's.

Jai Jai remembered how Father had carried him for miles. He really *was* super strong. Then Jai Jai recalled how super brave Father had been in the river's current when Father was teaching him to swim. Father also knew how to survive in the wilderness. He certainly was super smart, probably the smartest father in the forest.

"Remember the orphanage gate," Jai Jai whispered. "I know why I was left there. Some bears loved me very much. They knew a superhero like you would adopt me."

"My super son!" Father Bear raised his paw in a high five.

"My superhero father!" Jai Jai high-fived his paw back.

Jai Jai's mother came over to them. Then Father Bear and Mother Bear gave Jai Jai a big bear hug.

"Furever Family," Jai Jai whispered.

"Furever Family," Mother Bear and Father Bear echoed.

Jai Jai now understood Teacher Bear's wise words: "Fur is only fur deep. It's what's inside a bear that matters."

CPSIA information can be obtained
at www.ICGtesting.com
Printed in the USA
LVOW05s0927091215

465973LV00020BA/183/P